MW01069201

Ask your bookseller
for these other North-South books
written and illustrated by Coby Hol:

A Visit to the Farm
Lisa and the Snowman
Henrietta Saves the Show
Tippy Bear Hunts for Honey

Copyright © 1991 by Nord-Süd Verlag AG, Gossau Zürich, Switzerland
First published in Switzerland under the title *Taps der Bär geht zu einem Fest*
English translation copyright © 1991 by North-South Books, New York

First published in the United States, Great Britain, Canada,
Australia and New Zealand in 1991 by North-South Books,
an imprint of Nord-Süd Verlag AG, Gossau Zürich, Switzerland.

Library of Congress Cataloging-in-Publication Data
Hol, Coby.
[Taps der Bär geht zu einem Fest. English]
Tippy Bear goes to a party/story and pictures by Coby Hol.
Translation of: Taps der Bär geht zu einem Fest.
Summary: Tippy Bear and his mother make a clown costume for him to
wear to his class party.
ISBN 1-55858-129-4
1. Bears—Fiction.   2. Parties—Fiction.   3. Clowns—Fiction.
I. Title.
PZ7.H688T1   1991
[E]—dc20   91-8167

British Library Cataloguing in Publication Data

Hol, Coby 1943–
Tippy bear goes to a party.
I. Title   II. [Taps der Bär geht zu einem Fest]. *English*
833.914 [J]

ISBN 1-55858-129-4

1 3 5 7 9 10 8 6 4 2

Printed in Belgium

Tippy Bear
Goes to a Party

Written and Illustrated by
Coby Hol

North-South Books
New York

Tippy Bear was very excited when he came home from school.

"We're going to have a party next week!" he said to his mother. "Everyone can dress up. Can you help me make a costume?"

"Of course," she said. "We can make it together."

Tippy decided that he would be a clown.

He went with his mother to buy the fabric to make his costume.

"I like this one," he said.

"I like it too," said his mother. "I'll walk you to school. When you get home we can start working."

When Tippy came home his mother was sitting at her sewing machine.

"You've started working already!" Tippy said excitedly. "Can I watch?"

"Yes," said his mother, "I should be finished very soon."

Tippy had to try on the costume several
times.

"Why do I have to stand so still?" he asked
impatiently.

"Because this doesn't fit properly," his
mother explained gently. "I want you to have
the best costume at the party."

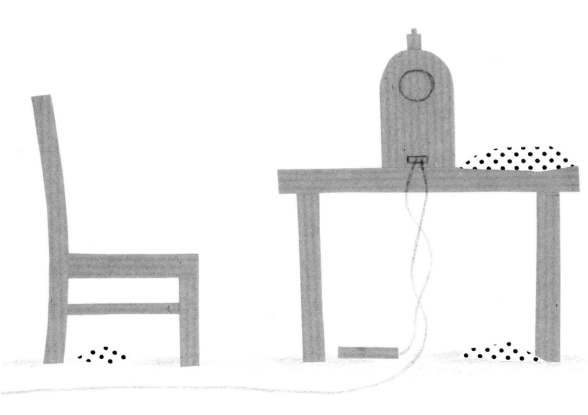

The next day, Tippy and his mother went
to a shop that sold masks, funny hats, and fake
beards.

Tippy put on various disguises.

"Do you recognize me?" he asked
his mother.

Finally, the day of the party arrived.

Tippy walked to school, wondering what all his friends would look like. He was wearing his clown costume and a bright red nose.

It was a wonderful party!
Everyone danced, sang songs and
played games.

Three of the older girls marched around twirling batons.

"I'm going to learn how to do that one day," thought Tippy.

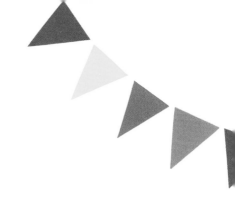

It was time to rest. Tippy sat on the floor
and drank a glass of cool lemonade.

When the party was over, everyone was given a balloon to take home.

As he walked along, Tippy held the string tightly so the balloon wouldn't fly away.

"How was the party?" asked Tippy's mother.

"Lots of fun!" said Tippy excitedly. "Everyone said I had the best costume."

"I have a surprise for you," said his mother. "Look in your room."

Sitting on his bed was a little doll wearing
a clown costume. It looked just like Tippy!